I'M A BOY BUT....

Nicholas Rabon

FIRST EDITION

Dedicated to my loving Mother.

I am a boy but....

I like to play dress up.

I sometimes like to pretend that I am a Princess.

I am a boy but....

I like to play with dolls.

I pretend that they are movie stars filming a Hollywood movie.

I am a boy but....

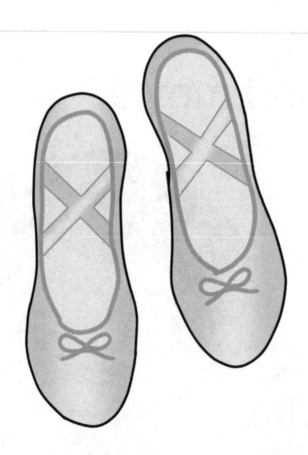

I love to dance.

I pretend my room is a stage and I am putting on a show for all of my friends.

I am a boy but....

I love to cook.

My mom lets me help her in the kitchen. She said one day I can learn all of the family's secret recipes.

I am a boy but....

When I grow up
I hope to work in
fashion.

I want to make really
cool clothes.

I am a boy but....

I sometimes get into
my mom's make up.

When I once accidentally got lipstick all over, my mom came in and laughed.

I am a boy but....

I wear my mom's high heels.

I strut around the living room and try not to trip.

I'm a boy but….

What I play with does not define who I am.

CPSIA information can be obtained
at www.ICGtesting.com
Printed in the USA
LVHW060427210519
618457LV00017B/294/P

9 780578 505237